JANE YOLEN

ILLUSTRATIONS BY
LOUISE AUGUST

MUSICAL ARRANGEMENTS BY
ADAM STEMPLE

G. P. PUTNAM'S SONS · NEW YORK

MILK AND HONEY

A Year of Jewish Holidays

To the memory of my parents,
Will and Isabelle Yolen,
and the years they made sweet.

J.Y.

To Alon and Caitlin
and to a little boy who is on the way
but does not yet have a name.

LOVE,
L.A.

Special thanks to:
Barbara Diamond Goldin, Linda Mannheim, Arthur Levine,
Rabbi Philip Graubert, and Rabbi Yechiael Lander.

Text copyright © 1996 by Jane Yolen
Illustrations copyright © 1996 by Louise August
Musical arrangements copyright © 1996 by Adam Stemple
All rights reserved. This book, or parts thereof, may not be reproduced
in any form without permission in writing from the publisher.
G. P. Putnam's Sons, a division of The Putnam & Grosset Group,
200 Madison Avenue, New York, NY 10016.
G. P. Putnam's Sons, Reg. U.S. Pat. & Tm. Off.
Published simultaneously in Canada.
Printed in Hong Kong by South China Printing Co. (1988) Ltd.
Book design by Jackie Schuman and Donna Mark.
Text set in Berkley Medium.
The illustrations are linoleum cuts,
on rice paper, painted in full-color oils.

Library of Congress Cataloging-in-Publication Data
Yolen, Jane. Milk and honey : a year of Jewish holidays / Jane Yolen ;
illustrations by Louise August : musical arrangements by Adam Stemple.
p.   cm. Includes index. 1. Fasts and feasts—Judaism—Juvenile literature.
2. Judaism—Customs and practices—Juvenile literature.
3. Fasts and feasts—Judaism—Legends. 4. Legends, Jewish.
5. Fasts and feasts—Judaism—Songs and music. [1. Fasts and feasts—
Judaism. 2. Judaism—Customs and practices. 3. Folklore, Jewish.]
I. August, Louise, ill. II. Stemple, Adam. III. Title.
BM690.Y65 1995 296.4'3—dc20 93-44474 CIP AC
ISBN 0-399-22652-4   10 9 8 7 6 5 4 3

CONTENTS

Thou shalt love the Lord, thy God,
with all thy heart, with all thy soul,
and with all thy might.
And these words,
which I command thee this day,
shall be upon thy heart.
Thou shalt teach them diligently
unto thy children, and shalt speak
of them when thou sittest in thy house,
when thou walkest by the way,
when thou liest down,
and when thou risest up.

—from the Union Prayer Book

ABOUT THE JEWISH HOLIDAYS

What is a Jew?

A Jew can be brown-haired or black-haired or red-headed or blonde. A Jew can have a large nose or a small nose or a medium nose. A Jew may be light-skinned or swarthy-skinned or with skin the color of ebony. A Jew may be short or tall, slim or fat, young or old. You cannot tell if someone is Jewish just by looking.

Jews live in the United States, in Canada, in Central and South America, in Europe, in Africa and Asia and Australia. You cannot tell Jews by the country they live in.

What the Jewish people share is a history that is more than 4,000 years old, a set of laws, and lore. The history is set down in the Bible, or Torah, or the "Old Testament." It is also set down in other books, such as the *Midrash* and the Commentaries. The laws and customs and wisdoms are set down in these books as well, though how they are interpreted and how they are observed varies at different times and places.

Jews also share a common belief that there is only one God. The watchword of the Jewish faith, called the *Sh'ma,* says that clearly: "Hear, O Israel, the Lord our God, the Lord is One."

And Jews share a certain set of holidays.

The holidays are not all celebrated in exactly the same way by Jews of different countries, or even by Jews living in the same country. Jews of long ago may have celebrated the holidays in other ways still. Customs, like people, can change over the years and over the miles. Sometimes great catastrophes—like war or famine—may also make a difference in the way people observe their festivals and feast days.

But there are some things that remain constant. For example, all Jewish people start their holidays at sundown of the night before and continue until sundown of the holiday itself. The reason for this goes back to the Biblical story of the Creation: "There was evening and morning, one day."

Another constant is that the Jewish holidays are not based on the calendar used by modern European and American nations, but on the lunar calendar, which is based on the moon's cycles.

Since the Jewish year begins in the fall, on the first day of the Jewish month called *Tishri* (approximately September) when the harvest would have been safely gathered in, this book follows the order of that calendar. Starting with the New Year—*Rosh Hashanah*—and the Day of Atonement—*Yom Kippur*—there are historical pieces, stories, poems, and songs to mark the celebrations. The year's cycle is complete with a section on the Sabbath, also called *Shabbat,* which is celebrated by Jews every Saturday.

So—enjoy! As Jews all over the world say on Rosh Hashanah: *May you have a good and sweet year.*

THE DAYS OF AWE

ראש השנה
יום כפור

History

The first ten days of the new year—roughly falling in September—include the two holidays that together are called the Days of Awe. Days one and two are *Rosh Hashanah,* the New Year celebration; on day ten is *Yom Kippur,* the Day of Atonement. This means that in a period of slightly more than a week, Jews around the world spend time carefully examining the previous year, trying to decide in what ways they have not lived up to the Commandments, and pledging themselves to a better new year to come.

In the Torah, Rosh Hashanah is called the Day of Sounding the Shofar. The *shofar* is a ram's horn that can be blown to make a noise that echoes like the last trumpet on the day of judgment. The festival is also called the World's Birthday and as such is a joyful celebration of all creation. Some scholars think Rosh Hashanah was originally a Near Eastern coronation festival that slowly became a celebration of God the King, who created the world.

Yom Kippur is a very different kind of holiday. In Biblical times, it was a day of elaborate rituals to help the people atone for their sins. It was also the longest day of prayer and of fasting—a custom that has come through to this century and promises to live beyond it.

Celebration

The majority of customs associated with Rosh Hashanah take place in the synagogue. The blowing of the ram's horn is probably the most widespread. There is no explanation in the Torah for what blowing the horn means. Some scholars say it is to wake the slumbering conscience; others say that it calls the people to war against wickedness.

The blasts on the shofar are among the most amazing and compelling primitive sounds one can hear in a modern setting. There are three kinds of sounds the shofar makes. First, is a long, clear blast called *tekiah.* Second, there

11

is a set of three short notes called *shevarim*. Finally, there is a quick, staccato series of nine short notes in a row, *teruah*. The long blast sounds like a wild animal, but the quick, sharp notes are more like a groaning or sobbing.

The shofar is blown several times during the Rosh Hashanah service by members of the congregation or the rabbi. Bible readings on those two days include passages from the birth of Isaac and his binding, as well as the story of the prophet Samuel.

Some Jews make a trip to a body of flowing water on the afternoon of the first day of Rosh Hashanah where they cast bread crumbs onto the water as a sign that their sins are being cast away.

At home, after services, many wonderful foods are served. A special favorite is apples dipped in honey for—as Jews say—"May it be Your will to renew us for a year that is good and sweet."

Yom Kippur, on the other hand, is truly a festival of repentance and atonement, when each Jew asks forgiveness for bad actions and promises to set things aright, *now*. As Jews like to say: "Yom Kippur is the day on which God gets up from the throne of judgment and sits down on the throne of mercy."

The entire day is structured around five services, beginning the evening before with the *Kol Nidre* service, named after the exquisite opening prayer sung by the cantor, the ritual singer.

Yom Kippur is also celebrated with five restrictions, or *afflictions* as they are known. It is a fast day, so after sundown of the evening before there is no eating or drinking. There is also no bathing, no anointing of the body with oil, no wearing of leather shoes, and no sexual relations. No kind of work can be done—not even cooking or lighting the stove or oven. Of course, only the adults and older children have to fast.

When the services in the synagogue are over and sundown ends Yom Kippur, then a great, final blast on the shofar is blown. After that everyone goes home to a big feast and celebration.

THE WORLD'S BIRTHDAY

Trees like candles
Stand and wait;
The wind blows green flames.
We celebrate

The world's birthday—
Rosh Hashanah.
Light the heart's fire
And the world's awe.

THE DAY THE RABBI WAS LATE

It was Yom Kippur, the Day of Atonement, and the synagogue was full. There was Motl the butcher and Lev the wheelwright and even Shmuel the *shames,* who swept the synagogue floors. Everyone was waiting for services to begin, only the rabbi was not yet there.

Not yet there? How could that be?

The cantor was ready to start chanting the Kol Nidre. The choir stood restlessly behind him. The members of the congregation looked up the aisles and down, not believing their eyes. The rabbi was indeed late.

But he was never late to anything—not to any service, not to any meeting, not to any discussion of Talmud or Torah. Yet here, today, on the most important holy day of the year, his reading desk stood empty.

"Go," the cantor instructed Shmuel the shames. "He may have fallen. He may be ill. He is an old man, our rabbi. Find him."

So Shmuel hurried to the rabbi's house, but the door was locked. The only lights he could see through the window came from the flickering memorial candles on a table. Wherever the rabbi was, he was not at home. The shames hurried back to the synagogue to report.

Now the congregation did not know, as they waited, that the rabbi was indeed all right. How could they know? But he was well. Well, indeed.

A good, pious man, he had set out in plenty of time for the synagogue. But as he was hurrying down one street, he had passed a small house, a shabby house—not to put too fine a point on it, a very poor house. And from that house came the desperate and continuing cry of a child.

Ordinarily such a cry would not have stopped the rabbi, especially on Yom Kippur. Babies cry and mothers comfort them. But suddenly there came an answering wail from an older child: "Oh, what can I do? What can I *do?*"

The rabbi could not pass by. He was, indeed, a good and pious soul. He opened the door, bent under the shabby lintel, and looked in.

There was a girl, no older than nine or ten, with long, dark plaits and dark, reddened eyes, trying to comfort a screaming baby. But the more she tried to calm him, the more the infant cried. Not only cried, but screamed and wailed and screwed up his little face.

"Oh, what can I do?" his sister wept. "What can I *do?*"

"Where is your mother, child?" the rabbi asked.

"Gone to synagogue with Father," the girl said. "It is Yom Kippur, the most

14

important day of the year. Surely, Rabbi, you know that." And all the while the baby in her arms kept crying.

"Nothing is more important than a desperate child," said the rabbi. "If we cannot care for the least of us, we cannot care for the Lord God. Go to the synagogue, my dear child, and bring your mother home." When the girl looked dubious, he added, "I may be an old man, but I have not forgotten how to hold a child. I will rock your brother until you return."

The girl gave the crying babe gratefully into the rabbi's arms and ran off down the road.

The rabbi held the baby first on one shoulder, then the other. He tickled the infant's tummy. He cooed onto the soles of the baby's feet. He clicked his tongue and wiggled his ears and played peek-a-boo with his long, white beard until the baby quite forgot to cry and was giggling helplessly in the rabbi's lap.

Just then the mother returned, with her daughter right behind.

"Rabbi, we couldn't believe it. Oh, how can we apologize . . . and on Yom Kippur, too."

The rabbi looked up from the laughing baby and, smiling, handed him into his mother's arms.

"It is right," he said, "that on this day of repentance adults should weep when they think of their sins. But children, who have not sinned at all, should not be left to cry." And so saying, he made his way to the synagogue to lead his people in prayer.

—based on a story from Russia

16

BLOWING THE SHOFAR

Where is the man to blow the horn?
Out in the courtyard, feeding corn
To horses standing in a row.
Then who is to blow? Who is to blow?

Where is the man who blows this day?
Out in the courtyard feeding hay
To horses standing in a row.
Then who is to blow? Who is to blow?

I will blow, I am the one,
The shofar will sound when I am done.
But drivers in shul have all forgot
Which horses were fed and which were not.

The Lord will wait, this thing I know.
And when they are fed—*then* I will blow.

—based on a Polish story about
Rabbi Jacob Isaac, the Seer of Lublin

THE HERDSMAN'S WHISTLE

On the Day of Atonement, everyone in the village was in synagogue praying mightily. The sounds of their prayers mounted toward heaven.

In through the doors of the synagogue crept a poor illiterate herdsman who usually spent all his time with his goats and sheep. But so intent on their prayers were the members of the congregation, they did not see him come in.

The shepherd had never heard such prayers before. The beauty of them and their intensity moved him. But as he did not know the words—nor could he read them in the prayer book—he could not join in.

As day drew to a close, the herdsman brought a reed whistle out of his pocket and tenderly put it to his lips. Then he blew a tune that used to tell his sheep that, though night was near, he would watch over them. He put all his love and hopes and prayers into the song and when he finished, he looked around.

The congregation was horrified.

"You have defiled our sanctuary," cried one man, "to play a whistle, a toy, at this holiest of days."

"You have ruined our service," cried two others.

They shouted and they yelled, and they would have thrown him out, but their rabbi, the great Baal Shem Tov, stopped their caterwauling by holding up his hands.

"Oh, my dear friends," he said, "you have not repented today. Despite all your praying, you have not asked for true forgiveness of the Lord. This young herdsman, not knowing the words to the prayers you recite, blew his own prayer straight from his heart to the ears of Heaven. It is he who has opened the gates of repentance for the rest of us. Even for me." And ending the service, the rabbi took the young herdsman into his own home to break the fast, seating him at his right hand.

—a Chasidic tale

SUKKOT

סכות

History

Called Tabernacles or the Festival of the Booths, *Sukkot* (which literally means *booths* or *huts*) is a week-long holiday of rejoicing and celebration that falls four days after Yom Kippur.

Along with *Pesach* and *Shavuot,* it is a Pilgrimage Festival. It continues the story that began with the escape from slavery in Egypt (Pesach, see page 55) and the giving of the tablets of the Law at Mount Sinai (Shavuot, see page 67). Because it also commemorates the harvest, its other name is the Festival of Ingathering.

Way back in Biblical times, Sukkot was the most important Jewish festival of all, so important it was simply called "the festival." Pilgrims would travel day and night from all over Israel to come to the holy city of Jerusalem for the sacrifices and special rituals. It may seem odd to us today that a kind of Thanksgiving was such an important holiday, but in ancient times most Jews were farmers and so the harvest was the most important time of the year. Farmers even built little huts out in the fields so they didn't waste precious minutes or hours walking back and forth to their homes in the village, time that could be better spent gathering in the crops.

Celebration

There are three important customs that mark Sukkot. They are: living in the *sukkah,* gathering together four special kinds of tree, and rejoicing.

The sukkah is a temporary hut made of four walls and covered with tree branches. It is a reminder of the little huts farmers lived in out in the harvest fields. Traditionally each family builds a sukkah outside before the holiday begins and eats in it during the holiday week. Some families sleep in their sukkah as well.

The sukkah is decorated with vines and vegetables and gourds. And the roof, though it must shade the people inside, must also not prevent them from seeing the stars at night. What if it is raining? There is a saying that rabbis use: "Don't stay out in the sukkah if it will spoil the soup!"

Often a family will decorate their sukkah with things like hand-made carpets, tapestries, decanters, wreaths, and paper and berry chains. The point is to make the sukkah a beautiful—if temporary—place to live.

Four special trees: Branches from three species of tree are made into bundles: the *lulav* or palm, the *hadas* or myrtle, and the *arava* or willow are bound together in a fragrant bundle and set in a holder of palm leaves. The whole is called *lulav* because the palm frond is the largest part. The fourth special tree is the *etrog,* or citron, and its fruit—which looks like a large lemon—is used. *Lulav* and *etrog* are carried in a parade in the synagogue and are given particular blessings as a symbol of God's bounty.

Rejoicing: Friends and relatives celebrate together in the sukkahs. But other, even more special, guests are invited as well. These are known as the *ushpizin.* They are not living guests, but symbolic ones from the Bible: Abraham, Isaac, Jacob, Joseph, Moses, Aaron, and David. In modern times, Biblical women, too, have become the invited honorary guests: Sarah, Rachel, Rebecca, Leah, Miriam, Abigail, and Esther.

After the seven days of the Sukkot celebration comes an eighth and much more solemn day called *Shemini Atzeret* when there are prayers for rain. Sukkot is about the year just past, Shemini Atzeret is about the year to come.

Immediately following Sukkot/Shemini Atzeret comes a separate holiday whose name means "rejoicing for the Torah": *Simchat Torah.* It is the day on which the year's worth of reading from the Torah comes to an end—and begins again.

All the Torah scrolls are taken out of the special cabinet or Ark and given out to different members of the congregation. Then there is a great parade around the synagogue, with those carrying the scrolls in the lead.

In the evening there are seven different turns around the building; each time someone new gets to carry the scrolls. The members of the congregation reach out to touch the scrolls or kiss them as they go by.

During the day of the festival there are more processions, and then it is time to read the very last chapters of the Torah. After that, reading from a different scroll, it is time to begin the year-long process all over again.

HOW TO SELL AN ETROG

In old Poland it was the custom among certain Jews that before anyone bought an etrog for Sukkot he would bring it to Rabbi Eizel Harif. The rabbi was known to have a keen eye and a fine sense of smell and so could tell at once if an etrog was fine enough to be used. Furthermore, the rabbi was a man of honor. He neither lied nor could he be bribed. Everyone trusted him.

Now one year Rabbi Harif was not happy with any of the citron crop.

"No!" he said to each and every etrog brought to him. "No. Not good enough."

Finally one of the etrog dealers became worried. No one was buying any of his wares. Instead they were hurrying to the next town or even traveling many miles into the city for their purchases. He knew he and the other dealers would soon go broke. And if he went broke, there would be no holiday joy at his own house. So he went to visit the rabbi.

"Rabbi, what are you doing?" he cried pitifully. "Our children will not be able to celebrate Sukkot if we cannot sell a single etrog."

The rabbi shook his head. He did not want to keep the etrog merchants' children from enjoying the holiday, but he also could not say something was good when it was not. He could not tell a lie. He thought and thought and then he thought some more. At last he said, "Well . . . there is one thing."

"Tell me, Rabbi," begged the merchant.

"Give each prospective buyer not one but two etrogs to bring to me."

"Two, Rabbi?"

Rabbi Harif nodded. "Two. When I am asked which of the two is better, I will answer truthfully. You will sell at least one and I—I will not have to tell a lie."

And so the rabbi kept his honor, the etrog dealers kept their good sales record—and the merchants' children kept Sukkot in a way that made everyone, even the Lord God, smile.

—a story from Poland

23

LAMA SUKA ZU/WHAT'S A SUKKAH FOR?

With a lilt

La - ma su - ka zu / What's a suk-kah for?   *a - ba tov she - li* / Fa-ther tell me true,   *La - ma su - ka zu* / For it has no roof

a - ba tov she - li / and the sky peeks through.   *Le - shev ba - su - ka ya ki - ri Le-* / The rea-son is in far-off days When

shev ba - su - ka cha - vi - vi Le - shev ba - su - ka ye - led - chen,__
we were wan-d'ring des-ert ways, And had no roof-tops for our heads And

ye - led chen she - li Le - shev ba - su - ka ye - led chen, ye - led chen she - li.
on-ly sand for beds. The suk-kah will re-mind us of the days when Mo-ses led.

SUKKAH SONG

I will bring in citron,
I will bring in palm,
I will bring in pieces
of the oak and elm;
and the great green willow
by the river's edge
will not begrudge a branch
for my little hut.

I will bring in apples,
I will bring in limes,
I will bring in platters
of the peach and pear;
and the late dark bushes
in the briary hedge
will not begrudge berries
for my little hut.

I will bring in sweet corn,
I will bring in gourds,
I will bring in baskets
of yellow squash;
and the tangle of
rambling vines
will not begrudge pumpkins
for my little hut.

CHANUKAH

חנכה

History

The history of *Chanukah* (or Hanukkah, or Chanukkah) is somewhat different from other Jewish holidays as its origins are not lost in the misty past. Rather it is a festival that commemorates a great and important victory in a war in which the Jewish people fought against their Syrian overlords and King Antiochus, the Syrian tyrant. It is celebrated in late November or December.

What the Jews wanted was the freedom to worship in their own temples, to follow their own customs, and to celebrate their own holidays. They wanted to worship One God. King Antiochus was determined to force them to adopt other ways and to worship Zeus along with the whole pantheon of Greek gods.

The leader of the Jewish resistance was a priest named Mattathias who fled to the mountains with his five sons. There they organized a guerrilla army, later led by one of the sons, Judah Maccabee. Though they were few in number, the Maccabees—as they were called—were fierce fighters. Still, they were vastly overmatched. The Syrian army even had thirty-two elephants that marched into battles carrying towerlike shelters from which Syrian soldiers could shoot down arrows. But the Maccabees did not give up and at last won the war, liberated the great temple in Jerusalem, and drove the Syrians out of their land.

When the Maccabees went inside the great temple, they found that before retreating the king's men had vandalized and defiled it. They had torn the Torah scrolls, scribbled on the temple walls, and smashed all the vials of holy oil. It was a terrible sight.

So the fierce Maccabees became cleaners. They scrubbed the temple from top to bottom. They erected and whitewashed a new altar. But—so the story goes—they did not have any holy oil to light the temple's lamps. By accident, one man found a small, sealed vial of oil. It was barely enough to last a single day. It would be many days until new oil could arrive. Still, with great joy, the Maccabees lighted the temple light.

And then—a miracle happened. The oil that should have only been enough for one day kept the temple *menorah* alight for eight days.

Most scholars say that the story of the Maccabean resistance is true, but that the story of the oil lamp miracle is only a folktale first set down in the *Gemara,* commentaries on the Bible. But whether the tale is true in all its parts or not, it has come to symbolize two things:

1. that the Jews, though small in number, will prevail against all odds;
2. that the light of Judaism cannot be extinguished, and burns brightly even through the darkest times.

Celebration

Five things are common to any Chanukah celebration: the festival lasts eight days; candles are lit in a branched Chanukah menorah or candelabrum; small gifts, usually of money, are given on each of the eight days; the *dreidel,* or top game, is played; and many special foods, like *latkes,* are fried in oil as a reminder of that one special vial of oil.

The Chanukah menorah has nine arms, one for each day of the celebration and one for the *shamash,* the servant, or helper candle, which is used to light all the other candles. On the first night, the shamash is lit and then one candle in the Chanukah menorah is kindled from it. The second night, the shamash lights two candles, and so on. Special prayers are said blessing the Chanukah candles and the holiday. One of them goes like this: "Blessed be Thou, O Lord, who has commanded us to kindle the Chanukah lights." The candles are put on the Chanukah menorah from right to left, the way the Hebrew language is read; then the candles are lit left to right so the new candle is lit first each night.

Gelt, or Chanukah money or coins, is given to children each night, a custom that goes back to at least eighteenth-century Eastern Europe, and probably much further than that. Actual gift-giving is an American invention of the twentieth century, perhaps so that Jewish children do not feel left out at Christmas.

The dreidel is a special top that has four Hebrew letters, one on each side. The letters are

Nun
Gimmel
Hey
Shin

Originally these letters were the initials of Yiddish words that meant "nothing," "all," "half," and "put," the instructions for a game played with the top. It was based on an old German betting game called "Trendle," and was not introduced into Chanukah celebrations until the Middle Ages. Much later the letters were said to stand for the Hebrew *Nes Gadol Haya Sham,* which means "A great miracle happened there."

Latkes are pancakes made out of potatoes and onions grated together, mixed with eggs, seasoned, and thickened with flour, and fried in hot oil until crisp. The potato latke is the most popular of all the fried foods made on Chanukah.

LET THERE BE LIGHT

Mattathias was a candle,
In him God's word burned bright.
He stood before the altar:
    Let there be light.

And Hannah was a candle,
Her sons killed in her sight.
She showed no fear before the king:
    Let there be light.

And Judah was a candle
Who called on Heaven's might.
He marched into Jerusalem:
    Let there be light.

The temple was a candle
That soon was set to rights
And for eight days the oil lamps burned:
    Let there be lights.

MAOZ TZUR/ROCK OF AGES

With force

Ma - oz tzur - y' - shu - o - ti, l'ha na - e l'sha - bey - âh,
Rock of a - ges, let our song Praise Thy sav - ing__ pow - er,

Ti - kon bet - t' - fi - la - ti, V'sham to - da n'za__ bey - ah.
Thou, a - midst the rag - ing foes, Was our shelt' - ring__ tow - er.

L'et ta - hin mat - bey - ah mi - tzar - ha - m'na - be - ah
Fur - ious, they as - sailed us, But Thine arm a - vailed_____ us,

Az eg - mor b' - shir miz - mor, Ha - nu - kat ha - miz bey - ah.
And Thy word__ broke their sword__ When our own strength failed us.

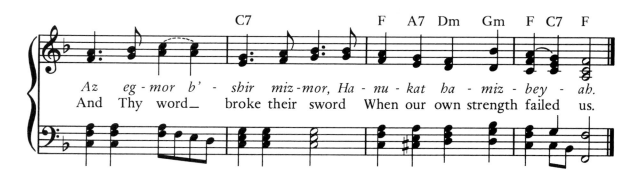

Az eg - mor b' - shir miz - mor, Ha - nu - kat ha - miz - bey - ah.
And Thy word__ broke their sword When our own strength failed us.

EVER AFTER

When I was four
and my brother Stevie brand new,
we lived in Virginia
with Grandma and Grandpa
only one long block from the bay.
My father had sailed off
on a great big ship
to go to war against Hitler.
But what did I know
about war, about Hitler?
All I knew was that Daddy was gone,
gone a long way,
longer than the block,
and we did not know when he'd be home.
"If ever," somebody whispered,
thinking I did not hear.
If ever.

Ever was a long time,
longer than it had taken
for Stevie to be born,
longer than it had taken
to move down from New York.
Ever.
Ever after.
And no one said *happy*.
When Chanukah came around
we had presents from Grandma
and gelt from Grandpa
and the dreidel spinning:
half for me,
take all,
give to the pot,
nothing
it should have said.
But I thought it read
ever.
Ever after.

Not one side said: *happy.*
I cried for my daddy then
and Grandpa picked me up.
"Look at the candles, Janie."
I looked.
"One a month for a miracle."
He thought to comfort me.
He thought I would forget.
But I marked the months off
one at a time,
'til eight were gone
and no miracle.
"Miracle?" asked Grandpa
when he found me sobbing.
He had forgotten
our Chanukah game
so could not stop my tears.
But in the ninth month
Daddy came home,
his arm in a sling.

"A miracle," I cried out
as he swung me up in his good
arm,
round and round
like a dreidel spinning.
"We forgot to count the shamash."
I knew then as I know now
a miracle truly happened there,
one long block from the bay,
one long year from the war:
gimmel,
shin,
nun,
hey,
round and round,
round and round,
happy
ever
after.

CHANUKAH SONG

With a bounce

O Cha - nu - kah, O Cha - nu - kah, Come light the me - no - rah!

Let's have a par - ty, We'll all dance the ho - ra. Gath-er 'round the ta - ble, We'll

give you a treat, *S'vi - vo - nim* to play with, *Le - vi - vot* to eat. And

while we are play - ing The can - dles are burn - ing___

PURIM

פורים

History

This happy spring holiday celebrates a terrifying moment in history when the Persian grand vizier, Haman, drew lots to decide on which month to kill all the Jews in the kingdom. The word *purim* means "lots."

The story behind the holiday goes like this: In Persia, proud Queen Vashti refused the king's summons and was banished by her husband, King Ahasuerus. A beauty contest was held to decide the next queen and a lovely young girl named Esther was chosen. Unbeknownst to the king and his council, Esther was a Jew. At the same time, Haman was selected to be grand vizier and he expected everyone in the kingdom—except the king and queen of course—to bow down to him. One man named Mordecai refused to bow since, as a Jew, he would bow only to God.

Furious, Haman convinced the king that the Jews were a stiffnecked, uncompromising people who had insulted the throne, and that as a consequence they should all be killed. The king agreed, not knowing that his new queen would also be executed under the orders he signed.

As it turns out, Mordecai was Esther's cousin and the two of them managed to trick the wicked Haman, enlisting the foolish king on their side, and saving the Persian Jews. And everyone—except Haman—lived happily ever after.

Whether such a thing actually happened—and many scholars doubt it could since the kings of Persia only married women from the seven leading Persian families—the story of Esther is a wonderful excuse for a joyous festival.

Celebration

The holiday begins with a reading in the synagogue of the Book of Esther. Every time Haman's name is mentioned, it is roundly hissed and booed. Noisemakers called *gragers* are used as well. Every time Esther's name is mentioned, the audience sighs, smiles, and cheers. People dress up in costumes, put on plays called *Purimspiels* that retell in amusing ways the story of Esther, and there are parades. Everyone eats and drinks much too much. There is a carnival atmosphere, a time of merrymaking and masquerade.

Cakes, nuts, fruits, bottles of wine, and the special three-cornered *hamantashen* cookies are delivered on decorated plates to friends and relatives. Money is distributed to the poor.

There is a large *seudah* or special meal at the end of Purim, taking place late in the afternoon. Purimspiels are performed at the meal, as well as parodies of readings from the *Talmud* in which verses are strung together that make no sense at all.

During the festival—especially at any of the parades—the merrymakers are always in danger of being hit on the head by paper or cardboard hammers or, these days, hammers made of plastic. No one takes offense and everyone joins in the fun.

YOM TOV PURIM/WE HAVE A DAY

THE GATEKEEPER'S TALE

Speaking Roles: Non-Speaking Roles:
Esther   Haman   Maids in Waiting
Mordecai   Queen Vashti   Other Guards
King Ahasuerus   2 Guards
(Note: Only Haman's part does not rhyme. That's because he is the villain!)

MORDECAI: I sit at the gate, I sit at the gate,
                I watch people early, I watch people late.
                I know who goes out, I know who goes in.
                I know every sinner and what is their sin.
                I write it all down in Hebrew and Greek—
                And a dozen more languages that I can speak.
ESTHER: Isn't he wonderful, isn't he great,
                Sitting and writing inside the king's gate.
                But what are you writing, dear cousin, pray tell?
MORDECAI: If you did all your lessons you'd know it full well.
ESTHER: *(Pouts)*
                I've learned all my Hebrew, I've learned my Greek, too,
                But the king will not want me because I'm a Jew.
MORDECAI: *(Puts his finger to his lips)*
                Hush, little Esther, and listen to me,
                You will marry the king and set all of us free.
                The plan is quite simple, you've heard it before,
                Let's start with the story right here at the door.
(He opens the door in the gate and they peer in, listening to what goes on between the king and Haman and Queen Vashti.)
KING: My wife is a beauty, there is no one finer
                In silken pajamas and black kohl eyeliner.
                Pray bring her before me so that I can praise her
                And, with all my compliments highly amaze her.
HAMAN: I go at once, sire.
(He bows deeply, with his three-cornered hat, then goes through a different door into the garden where Vashti sits on a lounger, surrounded by her maids in waiting.)
                The king wants to see you, Vashti, to pay you
                compliments and show you off.

VASHTI: (*Waves him away*)
            I'm tired of summons, I'm tired of whim,
            I'm tired of talking, I'm tired of him.
            Go away.
(*Haman goes back and whispers in the king's ear. The king stands up, furious.*)
KING: Put her out, throw her out, queen nevermore,
            Just like the rubbish, right out of the door.
(*The guards grab Vashti and toss her out the door, right in front of Esther and Mordecai who help her up and dust her off. Vashti stomps off the stage.*)
MORDECAI: See, little Esther, my beating heart quickens.
ESTHER: Yes, cousin Mordecai, as the plot thickens.
(*They turn back to see what will happen next.*)
KING: I have no more wife, but a king really needs one.
            So bring on four Persians, three Greeks, and of Medes—one.
HAMAN: It will be done.
(*He goes off into the garden and brings back the maids in waiting. When they stand before the king, Mordecai gives Esther a push through the door so that she is now on the end of the line of girls.*)
KING: (*Looks over the maidens*)
            Too tall and too tiny, too young and too old.
            Too sweet and too nasty, too shy—and too bold.
            (*He comes to Esther.*)
            But this one, a darling, I love you, my dear.
            Come tell me your name and please have no more fear.
            You'll reign as my queen, my delicious young beauty,
            Remember however, this one simple duty.
            Whenever I call you, then come here you *must*.
            That's not such a hard thing to take in, I trust.
HAMAN: Tell her the rest, sire.
KING: The rest? Oh yes . . .
            But if I don't call you, you cannot come near,
            Or else I will hang you, my darling, my dear.
ESTHER: A proposal unlike any other I've heard.
            But I'll marry you, King, here's my hand and my word.
(*The king puts a ring on Esther's finger and they kiss on both cheeks and hug. Then he sends her off into the garden.*)
(*A guard walks by with a sign reading: YEARS PASS.*)

46

MORDECAI: *(Peers over the garden wall and calls Esther.)*

Esther, my child, I've some news you should share,

Some men plot to kill Ahasuerus, I fear.

So if you can warn him, please do it, *toot sweet.*

If you're to stay queen, we need him on his feet!

(Esther runs and whispers in Haman's ear, who whispers in the king's ear, who whispers back in Haman's ear. Haman runs out and comes back moments later.)

HAMAN: The plotters have been found, sire. Mordecai reported them.

KING: Hang them with speed and write Mordecai's name.

To him acclamation, to all plotters—shame.

(Haman goes out the door again. Haman comes back in. Two guards at the door bow, saying, "Hail, Grand Vizier,/No one busier./Hail, Grand Vizier,/No one busier." But Mordecai pointedly does not bow.)

HAMAN: Mordecai—you may have foiled a wicked plot

But do you bow down to me?

MORDECAI: NOT!!!

I bow to God and to no other.

HAMAN: *(to the audience but not to Mordecai)*

Then I will kill you and your sisters, cousins, aunts, uncles,

father, mother, and brothers. And all the other stiffnecked

Jews in Persia. And I have just the plan.

(He goes in and bows before the king.)

Sire, there is a people in this land who do not bow down to you.

They do not believe what you believe.

They do not eat what you eat.

They do not celebrate what you celebrate.

Surely they must be killed.

KING: They do not believe in myself as their king?

How dare they, the heathens, do any such thing.

Here, Haman—my ring—you may do as you will.

Fix it all up and then send me the bill.

HAMAN: That's the beauty of my plan, sire, it won't cost you a thing.

We'll draw lots for the E-day. Execution day.

KING: What a man! What a hero! A leader! And wise!

You have risen much higher in your ruler's eyes.

(Haman bows and goes out, proclaiming through the audience: HEAR YE, HEAR YE, ON THE 13TH DAY OF ADAR ALL JEWS ARE TO BE KILLED, MEN AND

WOMEN AND CHILDREN, TOO. AND ALL THEIR TREASURES WILL GO TO THE KING.)

(Mordecai climbs over the garden wall and calls Esther to him.)

MORDECAI: Go quick to the king or he'll kill all the Jews.

ESTHER: I cannot go to him excepting he choose
To call me to visit. If I go—I die.
Surely you don't want that, dear Mordecai.

MORDECAI: As a Jew you will die, whether peasant or queen.
That's what Haman's law is now taken to mean.

ESTHER: *(She nods, puts her hand to her heart.)*
If I perish, I perish. I'll go to the king.
I'll wear my best dress, my best veil, my best ring.
I will plead for our people against this foul plot.

MORDECAI: A much better battle plan, cousin, I've got.

(He whispers to her and she smiles.)

(Esther puts her hands over her head and her maidens put a gown over whatever costume she is now wearing. She puts on a veil and she places a big ring on her finger. Then she goes into the throne room.)

KING: What—come to me summonsless—do you want death?
But you're such a beauty, you quite take my breath.
I forgive you, my darling, this one time, no more.
So—what can I give to the girl I adore?

ESTHER: Let's have a party, an intimate dinner.
And just invite Haman . . .
(She says to the audience alone.)
That crafty old sinner.
I've made some new cakes that I call hamantashen
That I am determined to get you to nosh on.
They're shaped like your friend Haman's three-cornered hat.
I believe he will love my attention to that.

KING: *(Nods and claps his hands, then reads book.)*
I've sent for our vizier, and while we're waiting,
I've got some light reading you'll find fascinating:
A book in which names of great men are engraved
Who each have, heroically, our kingdom saved.

(The guards bring in a table and pillows, the maids bring in dishes. Haman shows up in a new coat, but his old hat. He sits at the table with the king and Esther.)

48

HAMAN:	I have great news. The gallows is built for all those Jews.
ESTHER:	*(She shivers.)*
KING:	Well done, trusted servant. And what can I give
	To honor a man who made sure I would live?
HAMAN:	*(To the audience)* He must mean me.
	(To the king) Give him a king's robe, a crown, and a noble to lead him through the street.
KING:	Good thinking, dear Haman, that noble you be,
	So go bring the man at the front gate to me.
	His name it is Mordecai, robe him and crown,
	Then horse him and lead him all over the town.
	His name's in this book, for he once saved my head.
	He's never been honored. Boy—my face is red!
	And when you are done, come back swiftly to dine.
	We'll keep the rice warm and we'll well-ice the wine.
HAMAN:	*(Leaves and brings Mordecai back, puts the robe and crown on him, and leads him into the audience, all the while growling out,* THIS IS A MAN THE KING WISHES TO HONOR. *They come back the same way and Mordecai goes back to the gate, but Haman proceeds into the throne room and sits down by Esther at the table.)*
ESTHER:	Our guest, Mr. Haman, is looking quite sad,
	But alas, my dear king, I feel equally bad.
KING:	I give you my word you shall have all you wish
	And a bite of the delicacies on my dish.
	(He takes her hand.) Speak, dear Esther.
ESTHER:	Oh King Ahasuerus, I ask for my life
	That I may remain your dear darling and wife.
	For I have been threatened. And my people, too.
KING:	I'll hang anybody who dares threaten you.
ESTHER:	*(She stands and points to Haman.)*
	Here is the man who would kill me.
HAMAN:	*(squeaking)* Me?
ESTHER:	YOU!
KING:	And what is the reason?
ESTHER:	*(proudly)* Because I'm a Jew.
	And the man you just honored, who once saved your life,
	He's a Jew just as well as your dear, loving wife.

KING: *(Rips the ring from Haman's hand)*
These Jews are my friends for I owe them my life.
And also I owe them my favorite wife.
So, it's you—wicked Haman—whose neck will be stretched
(He claps.) I want all the top royal guards to be fetched!
(The guards come in and bow.)
GUARD 1: A gallows awaits, we will hang him with speed.
GUARD 2: A fit end to hatred, a fit end to greed.
MORDECAI: *(Addresses the audience)*
I'll write down the tale while I sit at the gate
So once every year we can all celebrate.
We will cheer the fair Esther, bad Haman we boo—
And on his old three-cornered hat we will chew.
ALL: *(Holding hands, they come out and sing a Purim song.)*

51

A WICKED MAN

With gusto

O, once there was a wick-ed, wick-ed man And Ha-man was his name, sir. He

would have mur-dered all the Jews Though they were not to blame, sir.

O to-day we'll mer-ry, mer-ry be, O to-day we'll mer-ry, mer-ry be,

O to-day we'll mer-ry, mer-ry be And nosh some ha-man-ta-shen.

And Esther was the lovely queen
Of King Ahasuerus.
When Haman said he'd kill us all
O my how he did scare us.
O today we'll merry, merry be . . . etc.

But Mordecai her cousin bold
Said: "O what dreadful *chutzpa!*
If guns were but invented now
This Haman I would shoot, sir."
O today we'll merry, merry be . . . etc.

The guest of honor he shall be
This clever Mr. Smarty.
And high above us he shall swing
At a little hanging party.
O today we'll merry, merry be . . . etc.

Of all his cruel and unkind ways
This little joke did cure him.
And don't forget we owe him thanks
For this jolly feast of Purim.
O today we'll merry, merry be . . . etc.

PESACH

פסח

History

Pesach (or Passover) celebrates the Exodus, when the Israelites escaped slavery in Egypt in approximately the 13th century B.C.E. It is a popular story. Pharaoh, the ruler of Egypt, refused Moses's request to let the Israelites leave and so was visited by God with ten plagues. These plagues included frogs, flies, boils—even rivers of blood. Finally, when the first born son of every Egyptian household—including Pharaoh's own son—died mysteriously on one night, Pharaoh let the people go. They left so quickly, they did not even take time to let the bread rise. However since the Israelites were such good slaves, Pharaoh changed his mind, and he sent his army after them. With God's help, Moses parted the Red Sea to let the Israelites through, but the waters closed over the following Egyptian army and the troops were all drowned.

Other names for the holiday are "Season of Liberation" and "Holiday of the Unleavened Bread."

Celebration

The three most important parts of the Pesach celebration are the cleansing of the house of all leavened materials, the retelling of the story of Exodus, and the eating of *matzoh* (unleavened bread). Some people use special dishes and utensils with which to eat their meals during Pesach. In Eastern European households, children used to take candles and go from room to room searching for crumbs of bread. They would look everywhere—in cupboards, under beds, behind sofas. Some families still include this as part of their celebration.

The focus of the Pesach festival, though, is the ritual meal called the *seder*. The word literally means "order" because there is a very special order or sequence to it, including the eating of matzoh and particular ritual foods. The matzoh sits on its own plate, usually covered with a special cloth. On another platter are the rest of the Passover symbols: a shank of a roasted lamb as a reminder of the

sacrifices to God; a roasted egg to recall spring when new life begins; *charoset*, a mixture of chopped apples and nuts and wine that looks like the mortar for bricks and so suggests the hard labor in Egypt; the bitter herb (usually horseradish) to recollect the bitterness of slavery; salt water to recall the slaves' tears; and a green vegetable—usually parsley—as a sign of hope.

The table is set with a cup of wine and a *Haggadah* at each place, though children only drink grape juice. The Haggadah is a special book that recounts the story of the Exodus and is a guide to the seder. It also includes stories, prayers, instructions, and songs. Some Haggadahs are exquisitely illustrated; some are even made specifically for children. There is also a place setting at which no one sits, for it is saved for the prophet Elijah.

At the seder, the youngest child capable of doing so asks four questions which—when answered by the adult leader of the seder—go far in explaining the reasons for the holiday and its many symbols. Those questions are: Why is this night different from all other nights?; why do we eat bitter herbs especially on this night?; why on this night do we dip parsley in salt water and bitter herbs in the charoset?; why do we recline at the table instead of sitting upright? (This last question has to do with the fact that in ancient times slaves had to stand during meals, or sit only on hard benches, while the slave owners got to lean back against soft pillows.)

56

Partway through the seder, the children "steal" a piece of the matzoh and hide it. Then it is up to the grown-ups to find the hidden matzoh, called the *afikomen*. Some say that anticipation of this game keeps the children awake and happy during the long evening. Others say it is to teach them that each person retains a bit of the child inside, looking to solve the riddle of the unknown. After a search, the grown-ups bargain for the return of the afikomen with the children. The children, of course, hold out for special presents. Only when the afikomen is returned does the seder continue.

There are four cups of wine drunk at ritual times in each seder. After the third cup, one of the children is sent to open the door for Elijah in the hope that he will enter the house at that time and announce the coming of the Messiah. Jews believe that when the Messiah comes, it will mean the end of poverty, slavery, hunger, and war.

After the fourth cup, everyone cries out: "Next year in Jerusalem!" That was a very special prayer when Jews were scattered all over the world, wanting nothing more than to return to the holy city. Now that anyone can go there, it is a prayer for the return of a special holiness to the world.

The seder ends with songs like "One Goat."

DAYENU

58

If God only made the Sabbath,
Made the Sabbath with its candles,
Made the Sabbath, candles, challah—
Dayenu

If God only brought us to the
Land of Milk and Honey,
If God only brought us to to Eretz Yisrael—
Dayenu.

Dayenu means "Even that would have been enough."
Eretz Yisrael means "the land of Israel."

CHAD GADYA/ONE GOAT

One, one goat,
    That my father bought
    For two pennies,
    That my father bought.

Then came a cat
    That ate the goat
    My father purchased for
    Just two coins.

Then came a dog
    That bit the cat
    Who had eaten up my little goat
    My father purchased for just two coins.

Then came a stick that beat the dog
    That bit the cat
    That ate the goat
    My father purchased for just two coins.

Then came the fire that burned the stick
    That beat the dog
    That bit the cat . . . etc.

Then came the water and put out the fire
    That burned the stick
    That beat the dog . . . etc.

Then came an ox that drank the water,
    That put out the fire,
    That burned the stick
    That beat the dog . . . etc.

Then came the butcher, who slew the ox
  That drank the water
  That put out the fire,
  That burned the stick
  That beat the dog . . . etc.

Then came Death to kill the butcher,
  Who slew the ox
  That drank the water
  That put out the fire . . . etc.

Then came God, so blessed be He,
  Who killed great Death
  Who killed the butcher,
  Who slew the ox
  That drank the water,
  That put out the fire
  That burned the stick
  That beat the dog
  That bit the cat
  That ate the goat
  My father purchased for just two coins.

THE PASSOVER THIEF

It was the day before Passover and a little Jewish carpenter was going home joyously for the holidays. He had been working hard, far away from his family, and he had three months' wages in his pockets.

The road to his village was long and narrow and wound through a deep, dark forest. Halfway in, he found himself face to face with a robber who had a very big gun pointed his way.

"Give me all your money," said the robber, "or I will shoot you."

"But it is the money I have for the Passover matzohs and the chickens and the wine for the seder. How can I give it to you?" asked the carpenter.

"Give it to me or die," repeated the thief.

So the carpenter turned out his pockets and gave all his coins to the thief. "Please," he begged, "at least make it look as if I put up a struggle."

The thief smiled. "What do you want me to do?"

The carpenter took off his cap. "Put a bullet through my hat," he said.

Laughing, the robber threw the hat in the air and shot a hole in it.

"What an eye you have," the carpenter said admiringly. "Now do it for my coat as well." He handed his coat to the thief.

The thief shot the coat right through the button hole.

"And in my pants," begged the carpenter.

"I have no more bullets," the thief said with a shrug.

"In that case, the devil with you!" cried the carpenter. And he pummeled the robber so hard, the thief fainted dead away. Taking back his Passover money, the little Jewish carpenter continued joyously on his way home for the holidays.

—a story from Poland

63

COME, ELIJAH

We were sitting at the seder
When my grandpa raised his cup.
He looked like he was praying
'Cause he rolled his eyeballs up.

So I looked up at the ceiling
Just in case God's face was there.
Then I checked again with Grandpa
Sitting on his thronelike chair.

He was smiling. "Come, Elijah,"
With a voice both deep and long,
Just as rumbling as the cantor's
When he sings a Pesach song.

"Come, Elijah," we all echoed,
Though our sound was weak and thin.
"Come, Elijah."
The door opened
And the neighbor's cat walked in.

SHAVUOT

שָׁבוּעוֹת

History

Shavuot began as an early summer festival called the Festival of Firstfruits when farmers from all over brought the first of their fruit and grains to the temple in Jerusalem. The word "Shavuot" literally means "weeks" and refers to the counting of seven weeks from the second night of Passover.

In the old days, men gathered in the largest towns and stayed up all night long. In the morning, carrying baskets of olive oil and honey, grapes, barley, pomegranates and figs, they walked in a grand parade toward Jerusalem. A special chosen ox led the parade, its great horns crowned with a wreath of olive leaves.

There was music—flutes and singing—and when the parade entered the city, the craftsmen stood up to greet the harvesters.

After Jerusalem's second temple was destroyed in C.E. 70, the festival changed character. Jews began to use the festival as a time to celebrate not just the fruits of the vines and the early grains but the giving of the Tablets of the Law to Moses at Mount Sinai.

Celebration

Both the harvest festival and the Feast of Laws are part of the modern celebration. It is either a one-day or a two-day festival. Orthodox and Conservative Jews celebrate on two days, Reform Jews and modern Israelis on one.

On the first night of the two-day feast, evening services are delayed until the first star appears. Some very religious Jews even stay up all night long studying the Torah.

Every house and synagogue is decorated with fragrant flowers—like roses—and leaves, and even small trees. This probably developed from the old custom of spreading sweet-smelling grasses on the floor, possibly as a reminder of the pasture at the foot of Mount Sinai where Moses brought down the Tablets of the

Law. Some scholars believe it may be recalling the olive-leaf crowns on the horns of the ox. Still others say it was because Baby Moses was found at this time of year in a basket covered with reeds.

The story of Ruth is read in the synagogue. It is a tale full of the sound of harvest and the smell of new gleanings in the field. The story is about Ruth who converted to Judaism to follow her beloved husband's mother, Naomi, back to Israel after Ruth's husband died. The two women were so poor they had to live off the leftover stalks of grain that the farm workers had not harvested. Ruth eventually remarried and took care of Naomi for the rest of her life. The story is a popular one because Ruth, the convert, was the great-grandmother of King David.

In many modern temples there are parades and baskets of fruits and flowers brought by the children. Often the temple is decorated with papercut flowers and trees.

It is traditional to eat dairy dishes on Shuvuot. *Blintzes,* rolled pancakes filled with soft cheese, are a special treat. So are honey cakes. This tradition of special foods stems from the Bible, which compares the Torah to "milk and honey."

Shavuot is also the time when children first begin to study Torah. There is an old tradition that Hebrew letters were written on a slate with honey and the children were encouraged to lick the honey off the slate, and so know how sweet the study of the Law could be.

SHAVUOT SONG

Egypt was long, Lord,
But for years we bore it.
The Red Sea was deep, Lord,
But still we came o'er it.

The desert was dry, Lord,
With no rain to love it.
Mount Sinai was high, Lord,
With blue sky above it.

Your face was too fierce, Lord,
For us to come near it.
But the Law is the Law, Lord,
And we will revere it.

WRITTEN ON A SLATE

Letters are sweet,
but sweeter still
is a word like honey.
Sweetest of all
the sentence that is Law
writ out on the world's slate
for the tongue to taste,
for the mouth to shape,
for each hungering soul
to have and to have
whole.

THE SABBATH

שבת

History

Unlike the other holidays which come once a year, the Sabbath—or *Shabbat*—can be enjoyed every week. It is the seventh day, the day of rest, and it begins, as do all Jewish holidays, on the night before. The very word "Shabbat" means "cease" or "rest," and it is a full twenty-four hours when all work ceases.

The fourth commandment is "Remember the Sabbath Day and keep it holy." For very religious Jews, this means that no fires are to be built in hearths, no lights lighted, no money exchanged or even carried. In fact anything that can be construed as work—like serious travel—is forbidden. So religious Jews live close to the synagogue so they can walk there each Sabbath for prayers.

Of course, since the Sabbath is celebrated by Jews all over the world, many different ways of observing it have grown up. With Jews living in large cities and spread-out suburbs more often than in tiny villages clustered around a single synagogue, many of the rules against travel have been relaxed for all but the most orthodox.

Celebration

Challah is a special white bread made on Friday before sundown. Especially popular are the twisted or braided loaves.

Candle lighting: Since the Jewish day is counted from sundown to sundown—or when three stars can be seen in the sky—the lighting of Sabbath candles before the dark signals the start of the Sabbath. There is even a special blessing that is used around the world, a blessing that has come down from the eighth century. Many families have candlesticks that are heirlooms, passed from generation to generation. Traditionally, it is the woman of the household who lights the candles and says the prayer:

Praised are You, O Lord our God,
King of the Universe, Who has
Sanctified us by Your laws and
Commanded us to kindle the
Sabbath lights.

Blessing the children: After the candles are lit, the man of the household traditionally says a special prayer, holding his hands over the children. In some families the mother, too, says this blessing.

Kiddush: This is another prayer over the wine cup. Traditionally, the man has said this prayer, but in the last half century women, too, have taken part in the blessings over the wine.

Blessing the bread: The challah is usually covered by a napkin or a special cloth until the wine blessing has been recited. Then the cloth is removed and the loaves of bread (usually two) are blessed as well. One explanation offered

for this is that in this way the bread won't be insulted because the wine has been blessed first. More probably, it keeps the bread warm.

Sabbath Queen or Sabbath Bride is the personification of the Sabbath, making the Sabbath into a person to be greeted with great joy and singing. Some Jews of the sixteenth century used to actually go out in procession to the outskirts of town on a Friday evening to greet the Sabbath Queen and welcome her into their houses.

Havdalah is the part of the ceremony that officially ends the Sabbath. When three stars can be seen in the sky, the Havdalah, or "separation" ceremony, begins. A special braided candle is lit. On the table sits an overflowing wine cup with a plate underneath it. Wine, candle, and a spice box called a *besamim* box are all blessed. Everyone takes a sip of the wine, then the Havdalah candle is put out by being dipped wick-end-down in the spilled wine in the plate.

As the saying goes: "More than the Jews kept the Sabbath, the Sabbath has kept the Jews."

THE SABBATH COW

Eliezer the farmer had a strong and healthy cow. They worked together six days of the week, but on the Sabbath they both rested.

For many years Eliezer made a comfortable living, but as he grew older, so did his cow. One day, he was forced to sell her that he might buy food.

At first, Eliezer's cow worked hard for her new owner. But he, not being Jewish, labored every day including the Sabbath.

When the Sabbath came, the cow would not budge. The new owner yelled at her, he whipped her with a stick, he cursed her name. Still, the cow would not move. Angry, the new owner ran to Eliezer's house.

"I want my money back!" he cried. "That cow is lazy. She will not pull."

"But she is a good worker," Eliezer said. "Did she not work yesterday?"

"Yes," admitted the new owner.

"And did she not work the day before?" Eliezer asked.

"Yes. And the day before that. But today she will not come out of the barn."

The two men went to where the cow lay quietly in her stall.

"There," said the new owner. "See for yourself."

Eliezer bent over the cow and whispered something into her ear. With a grunt, the cow got to her knees and from her knees to her feet. She walked out of the barn and stood by the plow.

"I do not believe it!" cried the cow's new owner. "What did you say?"

"I told her that when she was my cow, she was a good Jewish cow, and rested on the Sabbath as commanded by the Lord. But now she belongs to a man who is not Jewish, and will have to work every day, like her master."

The new owner looked thoughtful. "I see the cow knows better than I. I work seven days and have no knowledge of my Creator. I believe I will learn from this Sabbath cow."

He did no more work that day, nor on any Sabbath from then on. He studied the Jewish laws and became known far and wide as Rabbi Hanina ben Torta—Rabbi Hanina, son of the cow.

—a tale from the Midrash

SABBATH IN PARADISE

There was a rabbi who traveled from town to town teaching Torah. But this one day, the longer he traveled, the less he seemed to get anywhere. The path led to no city, no village, no town. Frustrated, he sent his assistant on to find the right road.

One hour passed. Then another. And still the assistant did not return. As darkness crept up on him, the rabbi became worried. It was almost sunset on Sabbath eve.

So forgetting his journey, he prepared for the Sabbath and began to say his prayers with such great passion there in the country air that every syllable went up to the heavens.

At first the rabbi's eyes were closed as he prayed. But for some reason he opened them and saw a man coming down the road toward him. At this the rabbi smiled. *A man,* he thought, *and where there is one man—there will be more. And where there are more—is a settlement.*

When the man got close, he said to the rabbi, "Will you spend the Sabbath with me, Rabbi?"

The rabbi answered simply, "Why not?"

"But you must promise me," the man said, "that when we get to where we are going, you will not ask a single question. In fact, no matter what passes before your eyes, you will not make the slightest sound. You must give me your word on this."

The rabbi thought for a moment. To give a promise when you don't know what will befall . . . *But I have no other choice,* he thought. So he agreed.

The man held out his hand and the rabbi took it. And they had walked only a short way when ahead the rabbi saw a wonderful palace.

The rabbi opened his mouth to speak, but the man put a finger to his lips. "Not a sound," reminded the man. "You promised."

And indeed he had, so the rabbi was silent.

They went up to the palace and the man opened the door. When they went in, the beauty of the entrance hall dazzled the rabbi's eyes and, for a moment, he shut them. But then he heard the high wail of a horn and the sweet voice of a fiddle—the rollicking sounds of a klezmer band. He opened his eyes again just as the man pushed open an inner door.

There was a temple, but more beautiful than any temple the rabbi had ever seen: adamantine floors and walls of alabaster and an Ark interlined with gold

76

and jewels too numerous to count. And marvelous, too, were the men who prayed in that magnificent room.

At the altar an old man with a long white beard recited the words of the Sabbath service so sweetly, the rabbi was entirely overcome. It was as if he were hearing the prayers for the very first time, so straight and sure did they go to his heart.

The rabbi turned to his guide and was about to ask him where they were and who the people were, but the man held his finger to his lips. "Remember your promise," his gesture said. So the rabbi was silent.

When the prayers were done, they went into a room even more beautiful than the first, where on a table of dark ebony wood were set plates and chalices of silver and gold.

The rabbi turned once more to his guide, but this time the man did not need to raise his finger to his lips, for the rabbi was silent and just smiled.

They ate and drank, they drank and ate, each bite and each swallow a revelation. It was as if the rabbi had never eaten bread or drunk wine before.

"And now I will show you where to sleep," his guide said in a low voice. Then he led the rabbi to a fragrant bed in a room in which the sheets were of satin and the pillows of silk.

The next morning at prayers, when it was time for the Torah readers to be called up, the rabbi thought: *Now I will know where I am, for each will be called by his name.*

The first was summoned: "Moshe, son of Amram, the sixth portion."

The rabbi began to tremble.

And the second: "David hameylekh—David the king."

He trembled some more.

And the third: "Shlomo hameylekh—King Solomon."

The rabbi was trembling so hard he feared he would fall down.

"Avraham ovinu—our father Abraham," called the voice.

The poor rabbi's knees were suddenly so weak he knew he could not stand. But, as he had been warned, he was silent. He said nothing, only listened.

As night fell at last, and the patriarch Abraham said the blessing to mark the close of the Sabbath, King David accompanied him in song after song on his harp. The rabbi felt tears falling from his eyes. But still he was silent.

Then a voice cried, "Quiet. The celestial council of justice is about to convene."

Hearing that, the rabbi gave a deep sigh. "Ah," he said aloud. Only that one syllable. "Ah."

The moment it was uttered, everything disappeared and the rabbi found he was standing alone at night in an empty field.

—based on a Russian tale

THE SABBATH QUEEN

Night hurried down our street,
Arrayed in her bridal gown;
In her crown three stars glistened.

About her feet, insects stilled and listened
To the Sabbath songs.
Father and I hurried to greet

The precious Queen of the week.
We sang as we hastened,
Our thoughts short, our prayers long.

This is where God and humans meet,
To drink the wine of prayers and sing
And each bite of challah is a blessing.

INDEX